# HANGEM HIGH SCHOOL

**Steve Barlow and Steve Skidmore**

Illustrated by Alex Lopez

**LONDON·SYDNEY**

Franklin Watts
First published in Great Britain in 2015 by The Watts Publishing Group

Credits
Series Editor: Adrian Cole
Design Manager: Peter Scoulding
Cover Designer: Cathryn Gilbert
Illustrations: Alex Lopez

HB ISBN 978 1 4451 4332 3
PB ISBN 978 1 4451 4333 0
Library ebook ISBN 978 1 4451 4331 6

Printed in China.

Franklin Watts
An imprint of
Hachette Children's Group
Part of The Watts Publishing Group
Carmelite House
50 Victoria Embankment
London EC4Y 0DZ

An Hachette UK Company
www.hachette.co.uk

www.franklinwatts.co.uk

The first day at a new school is always hard. But it is even harder when you're a zombie. Sam started getting ready hours ago.

"Breath? YUK! Oh, well. Maybe they won't notice."

"This is Sam," said Mr Broad.
"He's new. I want you to make
him feel welcome."

"Yeah, right!" said Clogger Mills, the class bully.

Later on at break time things didn't get any better...

"Let's have some fun with the new jerk," said Clogger Mills.

He put his foot out. Sam tripped over it.

*Oh, no!* thought Sam. *I'm going to fall apart!*

But Sam's new friends were fast.

"Why don't you leave the new guy alone?" said Danny.

But Clogger just laughed.

Then Lin had an idea.

23